"**D**ESPITE being aware of Hugh Ashton's many tales of Sherlock Holmes, and his *Untime* work, it was his superb collection *Tales of Old Japanese* that first alerted me to Hugh's real range, and his ability to capture character and mood far outside of Victorian settings. This present book, with its intriguing selection of short stories and vignettes, provides a further stylish glimpse into that range – from disturbing psychological musings, through witty horror, to what might be called modern weird fiction. Something for all tastes, with wry observation, an economy of words – and occasionally a lingering chill..."

John Linwood Grant, author of *The Assassin's Coin*, *A Persistence of Geraniums*, editor of *Hell's Empire*, the *Occult Detective Quarterly*, and creator of Mr Bubbles. Discover more about these and others at www.greydogtales.com

Unknown Quantities
Eleven tales of the slightly weird

Hugh Ashton

ISBN-10: 1-91-260563-5

ISBN-13: 978-1-912605-63-7

Published by j-views Publishing, 2019

www.HughAshtonBooks.com

www.j-views.biz

publish@j-views.biz

j-views Publishing, 26 Lombard Street, Lichfield, WS13 6DR, UK

Unknown Quantities

Contents

Unknown Quantities

Eleven tales of the slightly weird

Hugh Ashton

j-views Publishing, Lichfield, UK

Author's Note

THESE stories represent a rather different kind of genre from my usual 19th-century excursions, and were originally intended almost as "throwaway" pieces.

Some of them had their origins in exercises set by the Lichfield Writers group, of which I am a proud member, and to whom my thanks are due.

Sometimes only the first line was provided, as in "Me and my Shadow", sometimes the last, as with "Ships in the Night", and sometimes we were given just a basic theme, such as "Skip".

The Carnacki story is an attempt to reproduce the style and the feeling of William Hope Hodgson's stories involving the famous ghost-finder, whose cases were often resolved as being due to a mixture of natural and supernatural causes.

The other stories, including "Gianni Two-Pricks", are the products of my imagination, though John Linwood Grant, much to his bewilderment, provided the inspiration for this one with his talk of an anthology of 16th-century Genoese naval tales in the weird genre. Thanks to him for his support and encouragement.

Bee-bee

ANNE woke, unsure for a moment of where she was. The faint light filtering through the curtains reminded her that she was not in her own bed – or rather, she was in what had been her own bed until the time she had left home for college.

Since then, she'd been back home only a few times for Christmas or a family occasion like her parents' wedding anniversary, and she'd never stayed in their house. She'd always brought along her current boyfriend, and they'd flatly refused to have them sleeping together in the same house.

"It's not that we don't like him, dear," her mother had always explained to her. "And what you do when you're away from here is your own business. But your father and I won't put up with that sort of thing under our roof."

So it was a bed and breakfast down the road for her and Tony/Andrew/Phil/Keith and all the others who'd swept in and out of her life over the years. At the age of thirty-four, she guessed she wasn't ever going to settle down with anyone for keeps. Her school and college girlfriends, the few she kept up with anyway, had made nests for themselves, most with husbands and children, one or two with other women. The idea of having to share her life with someone else didn't appeal. She liked being able to shut the door of her flat when she got home, and exclude the world when she wanted. Company was only a phone call away if she decided to change her mind.

And when she thought about it, which wasn't that often, it had almost always been that way. As an only child, with her father often away on his business trips and distant from her whenever he was home, and her mother's busy-ness at the Women's Institute and the Mothers' Union and all the other good works, she'd been forced to make her own entertainment at home.

She'd never been good at making friends at school, and when she was about twelve, and she and her class had stopped being girls and started to become young women, she seemed to have developed the knack of making enemies without even trying.

She hadn't been a nerd or a swot, though she was comfortably towards the top of her class, and she wasn't the prettiest in any conventional sense of the term. But what she did have was some sort of power to attract the boys. Anne's hair and figure and legs could hardly be termed things of beauty when compared to the supposed boy-magnets of the other girls. Her face, as her father had told her more than once, was no oil painting, but it was hardly the back end of a bus, either.

Whatever it was, the boys had been interested in Anne in preference to the other girls. Anne had merely accepted this as a fact of life, and part of growing up, and had been surprised when the other girls started their jibes and name-calling, "Slut", "Slag", "Tart", "Prozzy" and so on. Which she wasn't. Certainly, she had enjoyed the attention and some of the cautious games the boys tried to play with her, but she knew when to stop them, and for some reason that wasn't clear to her, or even to the boys, they had respected her wishes, and stopped.

It hadn't been the same with Sally, Anne thought. The poor girl hadn't known when to tell him to stop, and he hadn't, and the result had been a pregnant fourteen-year-old Sally washing down fifty aspirin with a bottle of her father's whisky.

And then there was college, where she'd started going steady, if that's what you call a succession of exclusive boyfriends, but with none of them lasting for more than six months. And yes, it was all fun, but she kept coming back to

Bee-bee, as she had done for over twenty years.

Bee-bee was six months younger than Anne, and she had been given to Anne by her grandmother, who had died less than a year later. Anne had fallen instantly in love with the rag doll, who seemed always to have been called Bee-bee. No-one could remember who had called her that, or why.

Now on her fourth set of button eyes, and after many major surgical operations to repair almost ripped off limbs, severe abdominal lesions, and general old age, Bee-bee went everywhere with Anne, whether Anne was on her own or not. Bee-bee was always there to listen, sitting at the head of her bed, whenever Anne had doubts, or when her heart was broken as yet another man walked out of her life.

None of the boyfriends seemed to have minded. One even sheepishly brought a teddy-bear with him. "Didn't want her to feel left out," he'd explained, referring to Bee-bee, as he got into bed with Anne and placed the bear next to the doll.

She smiled as she remembered that night, and the feel and the smell of Andrew as they lay in each other's arms. She'd been touched by his sentimentality at first, but he had become a little soppy and ridiculous within a few months, so Andrew was no more, and Bee-bee remained.

It was the first time for years that Bee-bee had

been in this room. If Anne's father hadn't suffered a minor stroke recently and Anne hadn't returned to see what she could do to help her mother, neither Anne nor Bee-bee would be here. Mr Kenning had come back from hospital, and moved out of the master bedroom into the spare room where he slept by himself. Anne's mother complained that he was a bad invalid – always complaining about his treatment, his medication, and the exercises he was meant to be doing to avoid another stroke.

Her mother wasn't getting any younger, and it was a struggle to keep running up and down the stairs to take endless cups of tea, newspapers, books, and all the other things that her husband considered necessary for his survival as he lay in bed. And that was without the bathroom and all that entailed.

Despite all her past work on committees and in different groups, Anne's mother told Anne over the phone, "I'm terrible with these things, dear. I know we need to get some people in to help with your father, but I don't know who to call, or what to say to them when they turn up. So please come along and stay with me for a bit, won't you, and give me a hand with these things? And your father would like you to be here."

Anne doubted that last. She'd never got on with her father, and there seemed little reason to imagine that had changed. Nor had it. And as for giving a hand, it seemed as though she'd given both hands and her feet. Not that Mrs Kenning had given up doing anything, but she was so slow that Anne lost patience with her, and snappishly relieved her of whatever task she was carrying out, and did it herself in a fraction of the time.

And she had made the phone calls, but to no avail. For some reason that wasn't made entirely clear, it seemed that no help could be made available. Mrs Kenning appeared to give up, and left the bulk of the work of looking after her husband to Anne, who pointedly remarked at intervals that she would soon have to go back to work if she was to keep her job at the solicitors', and there was enough money in her parents' bank account to get some help in for a few hours each day.

"I couldn't do that, dear," her mother said. I don't fancy the idea of a stranger in the house."

So Anne stayed. Her firm very generously told her that they would keep her job open for her for up to a year, but naturally, they added, she couldn't expect to be paid during the time she was away. And with the bills from her flat still to be paid, and other expenses, Anne watched her bank balance slowly slip downwards.

So here she was, sleepless at whatever hour of the morning it was, lying in the bed in which she had hugged herself, pretending it was the new love of her life who was hugging or being hugged, or where she had cried herself to sleep in desperation at the loss of her love. And always with Bee-bee to listen to her. Bee-bee the perfect listener, who never got bored, never contradicted her, and always told her what she wanted to hear.

But now she was worried. Earlier that week, as she had handed her father his two slices of breakfast toast – one white with Marmite, one brown with marmalade, he'd said something really strange. At first she thought she'd misheard – the stroke had made his words somewhat indistinct – but however often she replayed it in her mind, she couldn't hear it as anything except "You look just like your brother when you do that".

Her brother? She was an only child. She'd never had a brother. But she wanted to be sure, so she had asked her mother, "Did I ever have a brother?"

"Of course not, dear. What a silly question."

"I mean, there wasn't anyone before me who died as a child, or... or given away for adoption or something?"

Her mother had shaken her head. "No. If anything like that had happened, we wouldn't have kept it from you. Why on earth are you asking?"

She'd made up some sort of answer about reading something about only children in a magazine, and her mother had returned to her

Sudoku in the paper.

Why would her father ever say anything like that? Was it just the stroke, or was there something more?

She'd had another shock the next day, when her father had asked for Nina to come upstairs to talk to him.

"Nina? Who's Nina?" she'd asked. Her mother's name was Alex, and the only Nina she could think of in her parents' circle was the vicar's wife, with whom they'd quarrelled some years ago.

"Alex, I said, tell Alex to come and talk to me," her father had said, as if he was repeating his order rather than correcting himself.

It didn't make sense. There was a mystery here, and she was determined to solve it. She slipped out of bed, and made her way as silently as possible downstairs to where her father's mobile phone was sitting in the living-room, unused since his stroke.

As she had imagined it would be, the battery was flat, but she took it upstairs to her room, and plugged it in to her charger. After a few minutes it started up and asked her for a number to unlock it. She chose 2-5-3-9, A-L-E-X, but she was still locked out. What about 6-4–6-2, N-I-N-A, then? Success!

She opened the address book to search for "Nina", and to her astonishment saw "Nina

Kenning" listed. Was this a cousin, or a sister or some relation who was never talked about?

There was no address, just a mobile number. Somehow it didn't seem to matter that it was nearly three in the morning. Her finger pressed the "Call" button, and after a bit she could hear the phone ringing. About five rings, and then a sleepy voice, Yorkshire or Lancashire by the sound of it.

"Peter? Are you all right? I've been worried about you. When are you coming to see us?"

Peter. Her father's name. Obviously his name and number were in Nina's phone. What should she say?

"Do you know Peter Kenning, then?"

"I should bloody well hope I know my own husband. Who the hell are you, anyway? And where's Peter?" A pause. "Has something happened to him? Are you from the hospital? How have you got his phone?"

Anne broke the connection. This woman was her father's wife? So what was her mother? And who was she, Anne?

The phone rang, startling her. The screen showed that Nina Kenning was calling. There was no way she could talk to this woman, so she turned the phone off.

As always, she turned to Bee-bee. "Bee-bee, I don't know what to do or say," she told the doll.

"How long has he been married to two women, and how many children are there?" She thought about her brother – her half-brother – whom she had never met, and probably never would. And were there sisters? "All those times he said he was away for a few weeks on business," she said to Bee-bee. "He wasn't, was he? He was with his other family. What have you got to say to that, Bee-bee?" A pause as the meaning of it all sank in and the fury built up inside her. "Bloody hell!" she whispered furiously to herself. "Who does he think he is, screwing up people's lives like that, the bastard? Not just me and Mum, but this Nina woman and her kid or kids." She suddenly found herself in the grip of an anger that she'd never experienced before. She was literally seeing red as her blood pressure soared and her vision contracted.

"What are we going to do now, Bee-bee?" But there was no answer. "Oh sod it all, you're only a bloody doll, aren't you?" she said bitterly, and for the first time in years threw her compan-ion across the floor, where the doll came to rest against the half-open door.

She started to weep silently, her head in her hands, crushed by what she'd just discovered, and at the same time consumed by an anger and a hatred that went far beyond anything she had ever felt before. "The bastard. The miserable little bastard," she kept repeating to herself, remembering the snubs, the put-downs, the barely veiled insults she'd had from him all her life.

I was only his second-best child, she though. Perhaps only the third or fourth. Who knows? And I thought I was the only one.

Through her fingers, Anne saw Bee-bee twitch. She rubbed her eyes, thinking it was a trick of the light, but there was no doubt about it. Bee-bee was moving, rising to her feet. Anne found herself unable to move, and watched, frozen, as Bee-bee staggered out of the door.

Silence. Then the sound of her father's bedroom door being pushed open, and ten seconds or so after that, a half-choked near-scream, which was suddenly muffled, and then cut off entirely.

Anne found herself still paralysed, and listened to what sounded like a quiet struggle, which went on for a couple of minutes, and then stopped. Without her having realised it, Anne's hands were shaking uncontrollably as she sat in an almost trance-like state. The shadow from the landing resolved itself into Bee-bee, who was dragging herself back into the room.

Anne suddenly felt herself move towards the doll, and scooped Bee-bee up into her arms. "What have you done, my Bee-bee?" she asked the almost shapeless mess of rags and stuffing. "And where's your eye?" as she noticed the missing button. The doll's face was torn, turning the smiling mouth into a jagged hate-filled sneer.

Half of her was aching to go to her father's room and see what had happened, and half of her was exhausted, and only wanted to curl up in bed and go to sleep.

Sleep won. She was asleep within a couple of minutes, and was only woken in the morning by the sound of her mother's screams coming from her father's bedroom.

"What is it, Mum?" she asked, though she was sure she knew the answer already.

"He's dead! Call a doctor – an ambulance – anyone!"

Anne picked her mobile – and dropped it. She'd picked up her father's phone by mistake. That would have to go back, and she'd have to make sure her call to Nina Kenning was erased. She used her own phone to call 999 for an ambulance before going into her father's room.

The sheets and bedclothes were rumpled, but her father lay there still and empty, almost peacefully.

"You're sure he's dead?" Anne asked her mother, though the answer seemed to be obvious.

"I'm sure. I saw enough when I did my voluntary work at the hospice." Strangely, she didn't seem too upset.

"I've phoned for the ambulance, anyway,

Mum." She put her arms round her mother, and hugged her. Both women were dry-eyed. "Now why don't you go downstairs and make us a cup of tea?" The traditional British answer to everything.

Her father looked much smaller than he had done when he was alive. As she straightened the pillow and tidied the duvet, she noticed something in his half-open mouth. With a feeling of disgust, she put her fingers between his dead lips, and pulled out Bee-bee's missing button-eye.

"Oh my God," she breathed, not wanting to believe the evidence before her. "Oh my God."

Now she knew she really did have to hide whatever was on her father's phone. Clutching the button in her hand and stuffing it into her dressing-gown pocket, she raced back to her room, picked up the phone, and rushed to the bathroom where she ran a basin of water, and dropped the phone into it, watching the bubbles emerge.

That should kill it, she told herself. She dried the case on a towel and slipped downstairs to the kitchen, replacing the phone in the living-room where she had picked it up only a few hours ago.

The doorbell rang as she accepted the cup of tea from her mother.

"He's upstairs, second door on the left," she told the ambulance men. "And he's dead. Excuse my mother and me staying down here, but we've seen him already."

They looked at her a little strangely, but went up, and came back in a few minutes.

"We're sorry to tell you—"

"Yes, we know. What was it, do you think?"

"Not up to me to make a definite judgement, but I would say a heart attack. He wouldn't have suffered much, for what that's worth. We'll have to take him to the hospital for an autopsy."

"If that's what you have to do," Anne's mother said.

When Mr Kenning had been loaded into the ambulance, and the cups of tea had been drunk, Mrs Kenning announced that she was going to lie down. "Just for a few minutes, dear, while I compose myself."

"Good idea, Mum. I'll do the same."

Anne went upstairs and closed the door to her room, making straight for Bee-bee who was waiting, as always, at the head of the bed. She picked up the rag doll, and showed Bee-bee the eye she'd plucked from her father's lifeless mouth.

"We did it, Bee-bee, didn't we? We did it together."

What you find in a skip

YES, I was frustrated and annoyed. We'd got on like a house on fire for the whole evening, and I was ready to go home with her, or take her home with me, when she looked at her watch and told me she had to be up early the next morning, so goodnight, thanks for the drinks and see you soon.

So I needed something to cheer me up. Didn't feel like the chippy, and we'd had an Indian together before we'd settled into the pub for the evening. I knew I'd had enough to drink – too much, if the truth was told, so that wasn't an option. And then it started raining, so I turned my up collar and kept walking.

It caught my eye from some distance away. A hand, sticking out of the skip outside the department store they were doing up. What looked like a woman's hand and arm, bare to the elbow. Visions of lurid headlines spun through my mind as I approached. "Lichfield man's macabre midnight find" was a good one, as was "Grisly garbage in city centre".

I actually laughed out loud when I got close to the skip. The arm was a mannequin's arm, plastic or plaster, or something. I pulled at it, and it came away, leaving me holding it like a trophy. "You look armless enough to me," I said to the now dismembered body in the skip. "Nice of you to give me a hand." (Don't worry, I get a bit like this after a few drinks. It could be worse – I could turn into a raving violent monster)

So there I was, walking back home, hand in hand in hand with my new friend (or part of her). When I got in, I put the arm on the table, and noticed for the first time that there was a slim chain round the wrist, which looked like gold. Not only that, but there were three pieces of glass, two red and one white, in gold settings halfway along the chain. Pretty, but not my style. I decided to take it along to my friend Julie who runs the antique and curios shop to see if she'd give me anything for it.

I left it for a few days, and took it in to show her. To my surprise, she didn't immediately dismiss it as junk.

"Where did you get this?" she asked, peering at the glass with a jeweller's loupe screwed into her eye. She sounded suspicious.

"I just sort of picked it up somewhere," I told her. Well, that wasn't a lie.

"I'm not going to take it," she said.

"Why? Not worth your while selling it?" I asked.

"Out of my league, dear. If I were you, I'd go down to Birmingham and go to one of those little shops in the Jewellery Quarter and see what they have to say."

And that was the end of that conversation.

As always happens to me with this sort of thing, I left it alone for a month or two, but one day I was going into Birmingham, and I had a few hours between meetings, so I decided to use the time to do what Julie had suggested.

I had no idea which shop to go to when I got off the train at Jewellery Quarter, but picked a small dingy little place – something in the way Julie had talked had made me cautious about going into one of the bigger more glossy stores.

The man behind the counter asked the same question as Julie had done.

"Where did you find this?" His tone was more accusing than curious.

"I found it on the street," I said.

"And you didn't feel you needed to hand it in to the police?" If the tone of his voice was anything to go by, he didn't believe me.

"A cheap bracelet and a few pieces of glass?"

"They're not glass." He handed the chain back to me. "Now bugger off, and be thankful I haven't called the cops. I'm not touching this."

I buggered off, as requested, the bracelet burning a hole in my pocket. The next shop I went to was a little more helpful.

"Hmmm... Two rather nice rubies and a very pretty diamond. Nice setting. Are you selling?"

"What's it worth?"

"I'll give you a couple of thou."

Wow. Two thousand pounds for something I'd found in a skip? Which probably meant he could sell it for five. "I'll think about it."

"Two five, and I'm not asking any questions about where it came from."

I had a sudden thought. "Tell you what. I'll give you five hundred if you do what I ask."

"Go on..."

ALL this happened fifteen years ago. The two rubies and the diamond now adorn my wife's custom-made engagement ring. And yes, she was the one who left me in the pub that night I found the bracelet, telling me she had an early start the next day. She really did have an early start, and she called me that evening to apologise for running away. By the time I'd found out the truth about what I'd discovered in the skip, I'd decided, and she was on the point of deciding, that we were going to get married.

The ring clinched the deal.

"How on earth did you manage to afford this?" she asked me when I gave it to her.

"You really don't want to know."

But what I really want to know is what happened to the person who threw out the mannequin with that expensive bracelet still on its wrist. Let me know if you find out, will you? I won't tell anyone else.

Babysitter

JAN didn't mind babysitting for the Coopers. They always left her something decent to eat, and told her to help herself from the fridge if she fancied anything else. One of them always gave her a lift back home if it was raining, and sometimes even when it was fine.

The child, Katy, was always in bed when she arrived, and never seemed to wake up, let alone cry. So babysitting there was easy. Nice big TV with Netflix, lots of DVDs to watch if there was nothing on there, even books to read if she ever felt like it, but she'd never even looked at what was on the shelves.

She was looking forward to a binge-watch of *Game of Thrones* when she arrived at the Coopers' but tried to hide her disappointment when Mr Cooper told her, "Sorry, Jan, the telly's on the blink tonight. Tried to get it fixed for you tonight, but they said the first they could manage was tomorrow morning. Sorry. I'm sure you'll find something to keep you busy, though. Make yourself a drink and help yourself to biscuits. We'll be back before eleven." And they were off.

She moped around, and in desperation turned to the bookshelves. There was nothing there that she wanted to read – not that she was much of a reader anyway – but a battered travel guide to Central Asia caught her eye. They'd been learning a little about the area at school recently, and she'd been interested in the story of Ghengis Khan and his Mongols. So... she pulled the book out of the shelf, and a piece of paper fluttered to the floor, with something handwritten on it.

She picked it up and read "Somewhere south of Tashkent" and a date about four years ago. She turned it over, and saw it was a photograph of the Cooper couple and ... what?

Standing between them was something that she could only describe as a cross between a chicken, a lizard, and a goat. It seemed to be about the height of a five-year old child, with feathers like a chicken but what appeared to be a dark purple colour, a head and arms like a lizard, and it stood upright on two goatish legs, ending in hooves. If it could be said to have an expression on what you might call its face, it was one of fear and terror.

She fanned the pages of the book to see if there were any more photos, but nothing else seemed to have been hidden there. She turned to the pages on Tashkent, and found a section describing tours of the desert that had been circled and underlined in pencil.

She studied the photo again. There was nothing else in the picture except for desert – sand and stones – and a range of mountains in the background. Weird. She put the photo back into the book, and put the book back on the shelf.

Time to check on little Katy. Jan went upstairs, and the little darling was safely asleep, smiling sweetly to herself, dreaming of whatever little children dream of when they're warm and happy.

She went downstairs and decided to make herself a cup of chocolate – the Coopers bought a better brand than her Mum did. It was one of her regular treats. It was a quiet night, and without the television turned on, she could hear the wind rustling in the trees in the back garden – and something else. A sort of moaning whining sound coming from outside. Just in case, she ran upstairs to check on Katy again, but she was fast asleep. Back down to the kitchen again, and the noise was still outside.

There was a torch beside the back door, and she picked it up, and unlocked and opened the back door. The sound was louder outside, and seemed to come from a shed at the bottom of the lawn, by the hedge dividing the back garden from the wheat field behind the house.

She approached the shed, and shone the torch through the window. Immediately, the moaning changed to a cry of despair, which sounded almost human. A face appeared through the glass, and she shrank back, recognising it as that of the creature in the photograph. Again, it seemed to her that the expression was one of fear and terror, and despite its hideous appearance, she felt a stab of pity for this – this thing, whatever it was, confined in the shed.

The door of the shed was secured by a padlock, but she remembered seeing a key hanging from a hook by the back door. "I'll be back," she called to the thing, though she doubted if it could understand her.

Yes, there was the key, and it looked like a padlock key. Back at the shed, she fumbled with the lock, and the door swung open. Immediately she was conscious of a dark shape hurtling towards her, and she was knocked onto her back as something – the thing – climbed over her. She attempted to grab hold of it, but it squirmed out of her grasp. Her nostrils filled with a foul smell, and she passed out.

S HE woke up in her own bed at home, and opened her eyes to see her mother bending over her.

"Thank goodness you're awake, dear. How do you feel?"

She went through a mental checklist. Did she feel all right? "Yes, Mum. I'm OK. What happened?"

"Mr. Cooper brought you back in his car. He said you'd gone into the garden and slipped over. You must have hit your head on a stone or something, he thought. I wondered if I should call an ambulance to check if you had concussion or something, but he didn't seem to think it was necessary. Shall I help you undress and get into your night things?"

Jan realised she was still wearing her clothes, but no shoes. "Don't fuss, Mum. I'll manage."

"All right, dear. Do you want a cup of something?"

"That would be nice, thanks. A cup of chocolate, please."

As her mother left the room, Jan's mind flashed back to the chocolate she hadn't made in the Coopers' kitchen, and what had happened afterwards. Had she imagined the thing in the shed?

As she lay there, she became conscious of something tickling her right palm, and she brought her hand out from under the bedclothes, remembering that she had made a grab for the thing as it had scampered over her in its rush to escape. She looked at the dark purple feather stuck between her fingers with horror.

Time thieves

H E woke to the sound of whispering voices all around him. Voices, but he couldn't make out any words. Just a rustling sound that made him think of moths, and other insects with large rustling wings, like mantises and cockroaches. His whole body shuddered with disgust under the sheets, and the papery dry sound suddenly grew louder and then stopped completely for a few seconds before starting again.

He didn't dare to open his eyes – he had a mental picture of his body covered with creepy crawling things, all legs and antennae and wings. He had to restrain himself from screaming at the mental picture. The reality would be even worse than the imagined horror, so he kept his eyes tight shut, and tried to ignore the sounds and the horror growing inside him.

The sounds were definitely voices, though, not the sounds that insects make, and he strained to make out any words. Whatever the language was, it wasn't English. There were far too many hissing sounds in it. What was really worrying was that the sounds seemed to come from every-where. There must be dozens of the speakers, all round him. This had to be a bad dream. At the same time, he was pretty sure that it wasn't a dream. Slowly he started to turn over, and once more the voices rose to an excited babble, then stopped completely. They started again a few seconds after he had stopped moving.

He cautiously half-opened one eye, trying to make out the digital clock that stood by the side of the bed. The figures showed 3:13, and as he watched, they changed – to 3:15. What? He must have read something wrong, or perhaps there was something wrong with the clock. He counted the flashing seconds, and after the minute had passed, 3:15 changed to 3:16. He sighed loudly, and the buzzing whispering sound suddenly stopped. He'd hardly noticed it while he was watching the clock, and the sudden silence was almost shocking. He waited, keeping still, and the buzzing sound started again. Without turning his head, he looked away from the clock, and thought he saw a pair of glowing red dots above the bed. Nonsense, he told himself. It's just an afterimage from the clock, and turned back to see the time jump from 3:16 to 3:18. There was no mistake. It definitely skipped a minute.

Even as he watched, two pairs of red dots

swam into his view, seeming to hover between him and the clock. They looked like pairs of eyes. As he watched, and his eyes became more accustomed to the dark, he thought he could almost make out dark shapes attached to them, almost like hummingbirds or some sort of large hovering insect. Disgust and fear fought against curiosity, and curiosity won.

He planned his next moves carefully. He could just about see the box of tissues next to the clock, and he knew that if he moved fast, he could reach the bedside light switch and grab the box of tissues with the other hand, almost at the same time.

One, two, three... and he moved. The rustling sound rose in pitch to become almost a scream, and he could see what appeared to be hundreds of small black shapes rising from the bed, and moving towards the ceiling, where they... simply vanished. One of them seemed to be struggling to fly away, and he quickly popped the tissue box over the top of it.

The screaming had stopped, but there was a frantic fluttering sound from inside the box. He got out of bed and slipped a sheet of cardboard that had come with a shirt under the box, with the thing, whatever it was, still trapped inside. He carefully carried it down to the kitchen, where he managed to chivvy the thing out of the box into a large glass jar, which he quickly closed.

Now he could see it clearly. It looked like a little demon out of a book – the sort with hooves and a tail, and bat-like leathery wings, about three inches tall. It glared at him with fierce red eyes through the glass of the jar. Even under the bright lights of the kitchen those eyes seemed to be glowing. The face appeared to be furious, and the mouth kept snapping open and shut, displaying two rows of thin sharply-pointed teeth that looked as though they would do some real damage if they came anywhere near you. He was glad of the glass between him and the thing.

But what was he going to do now? A minute's thought and he knew what he had to do. Taking the jar and its occupant to the sink, he ran the hot water tap until steaming water flowed into the basin. Carefully opening the lid, so that only a small opening – far too small for the demon to come through – appeared, he ran the hot water into the jar, ignoring the agonised shrieks and squeals that emerged. The little creature thrashed around in the water helplessly, seemingly unable to swim. As he watched, the frantic movements slowed down until they appeared to cease almost completely. Only a faint twitching at intervals showed that it was still alive.

He didn't want to touch it, but used a washing-up brush to remove it from the jar and place it in a zip-lock plastic bag which he placed on the floor with a chopping board on top of it. Without looking at what he was doing, he jumped on top of the board.

There was a sickening crunching sound, and immediately a vile smell filled the air. But that wasn't what caught his attention. The kitchen clock started to make a strange noise that he had never heard before. As he watched, the second hand suddenly raced backward at many times the speed that it usually went forward, and then stopped. It now showed the time as ten minutes earlier than it had been just a minute before. And as he bent to pick up the bag containing a red and green pulp, mixed with splintered bones and teeth and the remains of wings, he suddenly felt less tired than he had for months.

Ships in the night

H E woke with a start. Had he really dropped off? He thanked his lucky stars that the captain or none of the mates, or even worse, the boatswain, had not caught him with his eyes closed.

And talking of lucky stars... He turned his gaze to the sky, but the clouds were covering the stars. There was a faintly lighter parch of cloud which he guessed was where the moon was trying to break through. Looking forward, or after or to either side, there was nothing to be seen – just a wall of fog. Even the deck below his lookout post on the mast was blurred and hazy.

Well, that was why he was up there. The radar was on the blink – again – and the captain had a schedule to keep. So he was up here with his Mark I eyeballs, replacing the broken pile of ancient electronics that passed for radar on this ship.

The ship sailed on. He could hear nothing above the muffled monotonous throb of the diesels, but then he wouldn't expect to at... He looked at his watch. Surely it was wrong? It couldn't be that time already, could it?

It would soon be time for his watch to end, and he could slide into his bunk and sleep properly. He yawned. Stay awake, stay awake, stay awake, he kept telling himself. Only another fifteen minutes.

There was still nothing to be seen out there. The red and green navigation lights on each side of the bridge and the white light at the masthead above him seemed to show only thick fog. He hoped the radar had started working again. At the speed the ship was travelling, there'd be one hell of a bang if they hit anything, and he wouldn't be able to see it in time.

A thousand and one, thousand and two, thousand and three... How many seconds in fifteen minutes? It seemed like a long time – just quarter of an hour. Funny how time stretches and contracts depending on how you feel, he thought.

It must be time now, he thought, and looked at his watch again. Bloody hell, the hands hadn't moved at all. He held it up to his ear. No sound. He had no idea what time it was, but surely he should have been relieved at his watch by now.

I'll count slowly up to two hundred, he told himself, and then I'll try to find someone. He dutifully counted, and then, fully expecting to hear someone yelling at him from the bridge asking him where the hell he was going, slipped down from halfway up the mast and made his way towards the stern of the ship. There was no-one on deck, and as he passed the bridge, he looked upward. There was no-one visible. For half a moment, he considered the idea of committing nautical sacrilege and going up to the bridge uninvited, but the habits of years held him to the deck.

At last he reached the stern, and was shocked. Instead of the ship's wake streaming out in a straight line, it seemed to form a constant arc, as far as he could make out through the fog. As he watched, the brighter patch of cloud covering the moon seemed to move past the masts, behind the bridge. With a shock, he realised that this had been happening all the time, but his brain hadn't registered the fact.

There was still no sign of anyone else on deck, but he decided to make sure by walking forward along the port side of the ship, having come aft on the starboard.

Suddenly his feet started to slide from under him as he slipped on the deck. He could vaguely make out some dark stains on the wood. Someone's going to catch hell for this, he said to himself. He bent and dipped a finger in the dark sticky fluid. A metallic smell which he recognised as that of blood. What the—?

He shouted for help down the companion-way leading to the crew quarters, but there was no answering hail – just the endless throb of the diesels.

Then he noticed the lifeboat – or rather the place where the lifeboat had been. Now there were only a few splintered planks, smeared with the same dark blood. And the other lifeboat on the port side seemed to have been used to get away from the ship. The davits swung empty, the cables dangling uselessly in the water.

He tripped, and swore. The sky seemed a little lighter now, and he was able to see the hose that had fallen across the deck and caused him to stumble. Quite a lot thicker than the fire hoses, and it seemed to have lumps on it. Looking closer, he could just make out that it was a tentacle from a squid or an octopus or something similar, but many times larger than anything he had ever heard of, let alone seen with his own eyes. There seemed to be about ten metres of it, and the end where it presumably had been joined to the body was marked by a fire axe, buried in the deck. Bloody footprints surrounded the axe, moving in a pattern that looked almost like a dance, then skidding towards the rail, and then suddenly ceasing. There was no sign of whoever had made the prints.

He looked back. The wake was still curved. The ship still seemed to be sailing around in an endless circle. Now he really did have to get up to the bridge and see what was happening.

He climbed the ladder and stopped just before he reached the top. The door to the bridge was shattered to splinters, and was half-hanging from its hinges. All the windows seemed to be broken. Peering inside the bridge, he could see the floor was covered with shards of broken glass, and, as he had feared, there was no-one to be seen. Only one boot, which he thought he recognised by the distinctive pattern of the toecap as the second mate's, lay empty at the foot of the wheel.

The sun was starting to come up, and the fog was lifting – and it was increasingly obvious that the ship was continuing to turn. There was no way he was going to reach port unless he did something.

The bridge deck was slippery – not with blood this time, but with something dark and slimy which smelled bad. He didn't want to think about what it was, or where it had come from, but took the ship's wheel and turned it experimentally.

Nothing. Nothing. The wheel spun uselessly in his hands, and the ship continued her endless circle. He looked forward to the bows, and saw for the first time as the fog was burned away by the rising sun's rays, the wreckage and carnage of the ship's superstructure – and the nameless formless lumps of flesh, leaving red snail-trails behind them as they moved about the deck, following the gentle rolling and pitching of the ship.

As night turned to day, he started to understand the truth.

Carnacki at Bunscombe Abbey

"**A**s I mentioned over dinner, I have just come," Carnacki told us, over the brandy that formed the customary sequel to an excellent dinner at Cheyne Walk, "from a case that promised great things, and I confess that at the start I had entertained hopes of solving once and for all the matter of the missing Heptatrych of Laskaria, which would shed light on so many of the mysteries that have eluded us to this date. I may as well tell you fellows at the start that I regard it as one of my most spectacular failures, and one which will haunt me till the end of my days." He settled himself into the armchair by the fire, lit his pipe, and we took our customary places, eager to hear of his latest adventure.

"I had received a telegram from old Kirkwind, down in Dorset, requesting my assistance with a case that he described as being of possible interest to me, and being located at Bunscombe Abbey.

"The Abbey, as you are probably aware, is a fine example of a Jacobean manor-house, built on the site of a Benedictine Abbey, and full of secret passages and priest's holes, and the like. It has been owned since its beginnings by the Offley family, whose sympathies were always with the Stuarts. Indeed, there is a report that King Charles himself once hid there when on the run from the Roundheads.

"It is certain, however, that at one point in the Civil War, the house was occupied by three prominent Royalists in addition to Sir Edgar Offley, and was besieged by the forces of the Parliament. At length, possibly wishing to spare the hall and those women and children still in it from the damage that would certainly have ensued had the battle taken place there, some of the besiegers installed themselves in a wooden barn beside the manor. Rather than engage their opponents in a fight, however, the Royalists forces called on the Parliamentarians to surrender. On hearing a defiant refusal, they then fired the barn, hoping to 'smoke out' their opponents. However, the Roundheads, with the fanaticism of martyrs, preferred to be burned alive rather than be taken, and one of them shrieked a dying curse from out of the flames, prophesying that 'blood and fire will follow blood and fire'.

"Now, it is an extraordinary thing, but in the

generations that have followed, no fewer than four descendants of Sir Edgar have perished violently according to the prophecy. One was Captain Sir George Offley serving under Nelson, whose ship, HMS *Boscombe*, was hit by a French ball, and whose magazine exploded, leaving not a soul to survive the blast.

"More recently, Sir Joshua Offley was among those who perished in the tragic conflagration of the Hôtel Metropole in Biarritz some twenty years ago, and previous to that, two other Offleys have died in fires, one apparently caused by an overturned lamp in the stables – Sir Thomas died saving the life of his thoroughbred, Justinian; and the other death was the result of an incident involving a hydrogen balloon in the 1830s.

"Another curious thing is that, with the exception of the loss of the *Boscombe*, it has been the current baronet alone who has perished. Other members of the family have either been absent from the fires, or have escaped death, or even serious injury. It is not often that one comes across a legend with such forceful evidence to back it.

"When I arrived in Dorset, Kirkwind explained the situation to me. 'Sir William is not an old man, but as his physician I have watched his gradual decline, which has accelerated in the past few months. Though he is but forty-two years of age, his general condition is one of a man many years older.'

"'And to what do you attribute that?' I asked him.

"'It is this wretched curse business,' he said, and proceeded to give me some of the details I have just told to you, some of which were previously unknown to me.

"'But you say that this has only just come on. When did he inherit the title?'

"'Some five years ago and at the time, he pooh-poohed the story of the curse, calling it an old woman's tale. There was no indication that he believed in it, or took any account of it.'

"'And his wife?'

"'She died in childbirth some two months after Sir William inherited. The infant followed her some two days later, and Sir William has sworn never to remarry.'

"'To whom does the title pass should Sir William die?'

"'You shall meet him,' Kirkwind told me. 'James Offley returned from India some six months ago, and threw himself on the mercy of his brother, explaining that he had returned as a result of sickness contracted there. I examined him and was forced to conclude that he had indeed suffered from a tropical fever that had enervated him and sapped his strength...' Here, Kirkwind paused, and I encouraged him to continue, believing that there was more to come. Nor was I mistaken in this regard. 'James Offley had a reputation in certain circles in India as a reckless gambler, according to a cousin of mine who still lives in Calcutta. I was informed that he left the country owing considerable sums of money to some prominent members of the community there.

" 'In any event, he remains within the Abbey. I confess that I have hardly ever seen him, other than upon the occasions when I have examined him – his general condition, by the way, has neither improved nor deteriorated over the past half-year – and these examinations have generally been conducted in his bed-room. If I were to use a few words, I would describe him as a reclusive invalid.'

" 'And it is his brother, as the holder of the title, who is now concerned with the family curse?' I asked.

" 'I would prefer to use the word "obsessed" to the point of near-mania,' Kirkwind replied. 'Now, Carnacki, you may be wondering why I have called you into this business.' I confirmed this, and he continued. 'I find it hard to believe in such matters, but I have seen things that I cannot explain, and heard of more, and it is these things which have driven Sir William to the state in which he now finds himself.'

"Naturally, my attention was aroused by this, and as I listened to what Kirkwind told me, I was thankful that I had brought with me the Electric Pentacle and all the materials necessary to perform the Saaamaaa Ritual. To summarise what I was told, Sir William had awoken one morning some three months previously, to discover a circular burnt spot on the cloth covering the side-table beside his bed. He had no recollection of its being there when he had retired the previous evening, and on enquiring of his valet, the latter denied all knowledge of its having been previously there.

"Over the next few weeks, similar incidents continued, with scorch marks and holes burned into various fabrics in the bedroom. Moreover, Sir William, despite all attempts to dissuade him from such a course of action, insisted on locking himself in the room each night, with the only other key to the room being kept by the butler, Simmons, who stoutly maintained that it was always under his control. At all other times, the door was kept locked, save for the times at which the servants entered for the purposes of cleaning and so on. It therefore seemed impossible that any human agency was involved.

"As you can imagine, my first thought was of fire-elementals, such as the Aeiirii, as mentioned in the Sigsand Manuscript, and who are reported to leave a train of fiery hoofprints behind them when they enter our world, but for the most part, only one of these fiery traces was to be discovered on each occasion. I was, as I indicated earlier this evening, intrigued by the idea that these might be traces of the beings that are mentioned by Hermanius Magnus in his account of the Heptatrych of Laskaria.

"The effect of these continued visitations was sufficient, so Kirkwind told me, to drive Sir William into a state of near-insanity. As you might imagine, he was reluctant to enter his room at night, and when he did retire, it was apparently some time before he could fall asleep, as a result of extreme nervousness. All attempts to make him change his room were abruptly rebuffed, with Sir William claiming that the chamber in which he slept had been the ancestral bedroom of the Offleys since the seventeenth century, and that nothing was about to change in that regard.

"His valet had bravely offered to sleep at the end of the bed, in the manner of medieval feudal retainers, but Sir William would have nothing of that, and continued to sleep alone. However, his health seemed to be deteriorating, and he had the appearance of a broken man.

"'And only yesterday morning,' Kirkwind told me, 'there were two burned patches on the blankets of the bed when Sir William awoke, one of them mere inches from his body.'

" 'And he had heard or seen nothing in the night?' I asked. I was somewhat incredulous, as you might imagine.

" 'Nothing. However, I must confess that I have been clandestinely supplying Sir William with a mild sedative in order to help him rest more easily. It would be possible for a man who was already tired to sleep through such an event, though I admit that it would be unlikely that he would do so.'

" 'And what is the reaction of the brother, James, to all of this?'

" 'He has taken it very hard. If anything, he regards the family curse more seriously than his brother. He is, as I say, somewhat of an invalid, and these events appear to have shaken him.'

" 'And what is the relationship between the brothers?' I asked.

" 'Sir William has, in my estimation, been uncommonly generous towards him in providing him with a roof over his head, and, I may assume, been helping his financial situation in the past, though those days may now be over.'

" 'You have some basis for making these assumptions?' I asked him.

" 'Indeed I do,' he answered me, and told me that only a few weeks previously, he had overheard voices, seemingly those of the two brothers, raised in anger, through the door of James's bedroom.

"However, it seemed to me that there might be many other reasons for such an argument, and determined to ignore this aspect of the matter unless any further proof came to light. The idea of fires spontaneously arising was an intriguing one, and I asked Kirkwind for his permission to approach Sir William for permission to stay in the room overnight and conduct my research on the cause of the burnt spots.

"Kirkwind assented to my proposal. 'I am sure that as long as you do not intend to take up permanent residence there,' he smiled, 'Sir William will have no objection to your examination.'

"As it transpired, Sir William readily agreed with a sad smile. 'All your knowledge will be powerless to protect me against these terrors,' he said, sadly shaking his head. 'But if it will amuse you, I will sleep in the Blue Bedroom tonight, and you may occupy the King's Room.' By the way, the latter is so called on account of the story I mentioned earlier regarding Charles I's sojourn there.

'Well, dinner that evening at the Abbey was cheerless enough. It was hard to believe that Sir William Offley was a man of forty-two years. He moved and spoke like a man twenty years his senior. His brother James did not join us, taking a light supper in his room, and I was informed that this was a common occurrence.

"After dinner, Kirkwind and I sat with Sir William, who took but a single glass of port, and refused one of my cigars with an air of regret, claiming that the nicotine kept him awake at night. 'Lord knows,' he said to me, 'that it is hard enough for me to sleep these days, and I do not find that tobacco helps the condition.'

"My luggage had been carried to the King's Room, and I made my way there after bidding goodnight to Sir William, and Kirkwind, who was taking his leave before returning to his home for the night.

"It was a strange room, I tell you. The dark oak panels cast an air of gloom over the place, and the electric light, for Sir William had installed a small generator in the Abbey grounds, did little to dispel it. The bed was one of those massive affairs that you may see in museums – a four-poster with embroidered hangings, and appeared large enough to graze a herd of oxen.

"The furniture was of a piece with the bed, being made of dark curiously carved oak. As I started to make out details of the carvings, which seemed to be of monstrous creatures, the electric lights flickered and then went out, leaving me in darkness, enlivened only by the faint glow of the coals from the banked fire in the hooded fireplace.

As I stood there, unsure of which way to move, the door creaked open, to reveal Simmons, the butler, holding a small candelabra with three lit candles. 'My apologies, sir, but the electricity does sometimes do this. Usually Williams can re-store the power within the half-hour, but tonight is his night off. One of the men has gone down to the Red Lion in the village, but...' Here the good fellow shook his head with an air of resignation before continuing, 'I trust that you will not be too inconvenienced this evening and that you will be warm enough tonight.' I took the candles, which somehow seemed to increase the darkness in the corners of the room, and proceeded with my preparations.

"After the initial chalk circle and pentacle, strengthened with garlic, the Electric Pentacle was obviously the first line of my defences to be established, and I welcomed the glow from its wards once I had assembled it. I performed the Second Sign of the Saaamaaa Ritual at each ver-tex, though if matters were as I suspected, and that the beings reportedly described in the lost Heptatrych of Laskaria were involved, the Ritual would have little or no effect. My faith lay in the Pentacle, along with the linen-wrapped bread placed in the 'Points' and the water placed in the 'Vales', and I determined to spend the night inside that, provided, that is, that there was no clear natural cause for any untoward event.

"My watch told me that the time was approaching ten o'clock as I extinguished the candles, after having placed a chair inside the Pentacle and seated myself upon it. I confess that I had no idea what to expect but I strained with all my senses to detect anything untoward.

"I should mention that the night was a blustery one. The moaning of wind in the trees outside in the park tended to mask fainter sounds, and the shadows of the carvings on the oak chests seemed to dance as the fire died in the grate. It promised to be a long and lonely vigil, and I nearly dropped off to sleep several times, but the sudden rattle of rain against the window-panes at intervals caused me to start fully awake each time.

"At one point in that long night, I felt the 'creep' come down my back. Though not infallible, as you are aware, it is usually a sign that something unusual is about to happen, and so it was on this occasion. I was aware of a low droning sound, not unpleasant, but unmistakably eerie, and out of the corner of my eye, I saw a flash of light appear from the bed, and turning to look at it, I saw a flame, bright orange, burning fiercely straight upwards. For about ten seconds, as far as I could judge, the flame burned, and then shrank down into itself before going out completely, leaving the room in almost complete darkness.

Like a fool, I had neglected to check the charge of the Pentacle, which was by now growing dim. Quite frankly, I was in a funk. How could such a flame rise up spontaneously, and just as quickly, extinguish itself? I was aware of a faint acrid smell, which was unlike the remembered smell of burned cloth, and which puzzled me, but I had no wish to get up and examine the matter any further.

"I waited, my nerves on edge, until the sound of birdsong and a faint glow of light from behind the curtains informed me that morning had come. I left the Pentacle and drew back the hangings, showing me the burned hole in the bedclothes where the flame had shone. There was no trace of what had happened, other than a ring of charred material, with a black charred centre. The flame appeared to have burned through the two outer blankets, but not the third, but still I shuddered to think that this was close to where Sir William would have slept had I not occupied the room for the night. The acrid smell I had noticed earlier seemed to be stronger near the scorched cloth, but I was unable to place it. No visible cause of the fire could be made out, and my case for the Heptatrych of Laskaria seemed stronger than ever before.

"I cleared away my protections – though they had done little good insofar as the room was concerned – and performed the Assyrian Ritual of Banishing, paying particular attention to the bed, using the hyssop branches I had brought with me, and a little of the triple-distilled water that had protected me while in the Pentacle. I had given orders that the door to the room be left unlocked, and I made my way out of the room, to be greeted in the corridor by Simmons. I suppose that the effects of the previous night's happenings showed on my face, as he enquired after my health most solicitously. I reassured him, informing him of the scorched blankets, which I requested him to change, intending to keep this occurrence from Sir William, and he promised me that this would be attended to, adding that my breakfast would be brought to me in the dining-room within a very short space of time.

"On entering the room, I was surprised to see a stranger, clad in a dressing-gown, partaking of porridge. 'Forgive me for not having been present yesterday evening,' he apologised, as he introduced himself as James, the younger brother of Sir William. I introduced myself in my turn and felt compelled to give some account of my reason for visiting the Abbey.

"'Ah, a sad business, that,' he said to me. 'It's almost enough to make one believe in the old family curse. Have you heard the story?' I assured him that I had, and he went on. 'While

William refuses to have anyone else sleep in that room, we will never know the story of these mysterious marks.'

"I informed him that I had spent the previous night in the room, and he received this news with somewhat of a start. 'Can you say what you saw there?' he asked, seemingly taken aback.

"For some reason I decided to withhold the truth. 'I saw nothing of interest,' I told him. 'No doubt my psychical defences were enough to repel any untoward manifestations.'

" 'No doubt that is it,' he replied, and it might have been my imagination, but it seemed to me that there was a note of relief in his voice. By now my breakfast of kippers and eggs had arrived, and my companion had completed the demolition of a lightly-boiled egg. 'If you will excuse me,' he said, rising. 'I am somewhat of an invalid, and I must rest.' He left the room, and I heard him go upstairs. This sound was followed by that of the door to the King's Room being opened – a most distinctive sound that I had remarked the previous evening. I softly rose, and made may way out of the dining-room to the hall, where I could see up the stairs to the door in question. As I watched, it opened, and James Offley appeared, before moving along the landing, seemingly to his own room. I returned to my breakfast, lost in thought.

"It might be, I considered, that James Offley was merely expressing an interest in the strange goings-on that room, but I had assured him that I could tell him nothing of interest in that regard, and he had no reason to disbelieve me. On the other hand, he had displayed what might be considered undue signs of surprise when I informed him that I had passed the night in the room.

"As I was finishing my meal, Sir William entered, and greeted me with some warmth. 'I trust you slept well,' I enquired.

"'Indeed I did. I rested better than I have in some time,' he answered me, and indeed, there was a flush to his cheeks and a sparkle in his eye which had been absent the previous day. 'Did you observe anything of interest?' he asked me.

"Given the state of his nerves, I kept to my purpose of maintaining silence, and informed him that nothing untoward had occurred. I stayed talking with him for some time, until Simmons announced the arrival of Kirkwind, who entered with a start of surprise as he marked Sir William's improved condition.

"Following a brief conversation with his patient, Kirkwind proposed that he and I should take advantage of the break in the weather, the previous night's rain now having given way to bright sunshine, and walk to the village where a package from London was awaiting him. Clearly he was anxious to know what, if anything, I had observed, and I provided him with a full account of the previous night's happenings as we walked along the road.

" 'There is no doubt in your mind that these flames arose from some source other than our world?' he asked me.

"I contradicted him. 'There is always room for doubt in cases of this kind,' I told him, 'but in this case, the doubts are outweighed by my feelings on the matter. If, as I suspect, they do proceed from such sources, the rituals that I have performed should prevent their recurrence.'

" 'Then you consider that Sir William may safely sleep in the King's Room tonight?' he asked me, and like a fool I told him that Sir William would be in no danger.

"I cannot blame another for what occurred next. I had taken full responsibility in this case, giving my professional opinion, which turned out to be in error, and I must live with that knowledge until the day I die.

"Following dinner that evening, at which both Sir William and James Offley were present, together with Kirkwind and myself, retired to our rooms. Sir William returned to his usual quarters in the King's Room, his brother to his own room, which was two doors down the corridor from that of his brother, I to the Blue Room at some distance from the two rooms I have just mentioned, and Kirkwind, who had been invited to stay the night, to a smaller room adjoining mine.

"The Blue Room was decorated in gay shades of the hue that gave it its name, and was a chamber of more comforting and pleasing aspect than my previous night's lodgings. I need hardly mention that following the previous almost sleepless night, I was extremely fatigued, and it seemed to me that no sooner had my head touched the pillow than I was in a deep dreamless sleep.

"I say that it was dreamless, but although at the time I was unconscious of any dreams, I can now recall a vague fluttering of leathery wings, and a rustle of whispering voices, which now bring to mind the Aeiirii. The brain plays queer tricks, and it is possible, in the light of what had happened on the previous night, that my mind was in some way repeating the events that took place then. On the other hand... but I must not anticipate.

"I was awoken by a frantic knocking on my bedroom door, and the voice of Simmons fairly screaming at me, 'Mr. Carnacki! Come at once, sir!'

"I threw on my dressing-gown and opened the door to discover the white-faced Simmons, seemingly in a state of shock. 'I have just unlocked the

King's Room, sir, to bring Sir William his morning tea, and oh sir, it is a most terrible sight. Mr. Carnacki, sir, if you would please go to the King's Room immediately, I would be – we all would be – most obliged. And you too, sir,' he addressed Kirkwind, who had emerged, bleary-eyed, in the doorway of his room. Poor Simmons seemed to be almost at his wits' end. He was agitated almost beyond belief, and I noted his shaking hands as he held my door open.

"I need hardly say that I hastened to carry out his request, and fairly raced along the passageway to the King's Room, where a tearful maid was standing. One glance seemed to indicate that life was extinct in the body of Sir William, lying in the bed, and it took only a few seconds' examination by Kirkwind to confirm this.

"The expression on the face was one of horror mixed with terror. What was more ghastly, to my mind, was the presence of two charred circles, similar to the one I had observed the previous morning, but these were on the very pillow on which Sir William's head reposed, not six inches from his face.

"'Heart, I would say,' commented Kirkwind. 'It was never strong, and whatever caused these,' pointing at the marks left by the fires, 'must have frightened him to death.'

"'I see now,' said I, 'that all my precautions

and devices were in vain.'

" 'Indeed they were,' came in mocking tones from behind me, and turning, I beheld James Offley standing in the doorway, shaking his finger at me. ' "Blood and fire will follow blood and fire".' He quoted the old curse in an almost delirious fashion, his eyes staring wildly at the inert body of his brother. 'There is no escape from these things. Mr. Carnacki, you of all people should be aware of this.'

"His words cut me to the quick – I had failed, and failed abominably – in my task of solving the mystery and protecting Sir William from his fate. Kirkwind rounded on James Offley with a look of fury on his face. 'Out! Out, I say!' he cried, advancing on him and slamming the door in his face. I was astonished by his actions, but held my peace as I examined the scorched circles by the side of the dead man's head. Again, I was conscious of the acrid smell I had noticed before, but on this occasion I observed something that had previously escaped my notice.

"Around the edge of each of the blackened circles was a residue of a white powder which at first I took to be the ash of the fabric that had been consumed by the fire, but on closer examination with my *loupe,* it was clear that this was a crystalline substance, deposited around the scorched areas, and nowhere else. I called Kirkwind's attention to it, and he confirmed my findings.

" 'You have nothing for which to reproach yourself,' he reassured me. 'If these fires and flames had a supernatural cause, there would be no physical residue such as this, surely?' I was forced to agree with the truth of this argument, and conclude that there must be a natural cause for these phenomena. But what, I asked myself, could conceivably be the origin of the flame that I had indubitably seen with my own eyes only the previous night to last?

" 'There is only one who stands to gain from Sir William's death,' he continued, 'and I am relying on you to prove that it was he. Sir William was my friend, as well as being my patient, and I freely confess that I mistrust and dislike the man whom I suppose we must now, since he has inherited the title, refer to as Sir James.'

"I was more than a little shaken by the vehemence in Kirkwind's voice, but was forced to bow before his superior knowledge of the situation, and the personalities involved. Together, we prepared the body for removal from the room by the servants, and I took the pillow for further examination.

"It was now clear to me that more examination of the room was needed. I had hopes that I might discover some more of the substance, whatever it might be, that had left these deposits

on the pillow. Even were I to be successful, I re-
flected, I would still be in the dark as regards the
exact purpose of the substance, not to mention
the way in which it had been employed and introduced into the room.

"My searches were in vain. There was nothing
that provided an answer to either of these problems, and I left the King's Room, carrying the
pillow, and taking care to ensure the door was
locked behind me.

"I met Kirkwind in the library. He was shaking
with anger. 'The scoundrel!' he exclaimed. 'The
cad! His brother is hardly cold, and he is already
proposing to move himself into the King's Room,
and he is already styling himself as Sir James!
This whole business is intolerable, and I wash
my hands of the affair and of the household. The
man who calls himself Sir James Offley will have
to find himself a new physician. If you are wise,
Carnacki, I advise you to do the same as I, and
quit this place at the first possible opportunity.'
He swept out of the room, calling for his hat and
coat and stick.

"Well, that placed me in a pretty situation, as
you can imagine. I now had the bit between my
teeth, and I was determined to stick the course
to the end. On the other hand, Kirkwind, a man
whose judgement I trusted, seemed to wish to
distance himself from the business at hand, and

it appeared to me that he had some motive for doing so for which he had yet to provide me with an explanation.

"I shut myself in the library, emerging only when luncheon was announced, a meal that I ate in solitude. Simmons informed me that 'Mr. James, or perhaps I should now say Sir James,' as he corrected himself, had now taken up residence in the King's Room. I observed an air of disapproval in the way in which he delivered this news to me, but forbore from making any comment other than to acknowledge the news.

"It appeared to me as I examined the pillow that the white crystalline substance was familiar to me, but I was unable to place it, even after cautiously placing a few grains upon my tongue to determine the taste. At the same time, I was conscious of a slight stomach-ache, quite possibly the result of the strain of the recent hours. I rang the bell and enquired of Simmons whether there was any Phillips' Milk of Magnesia to be had. It is a remedy that I have frequently to be effective on such occasions. To my relief, he returned in a few minutes with a bottle and glass. He explained that Sir James suffered from dyspepsia, and that this mixture afforded him some relief.

"As I drank down the medicine, my memory was refreshed, and I could identify the substance on the pillow as the hydroxide of magnesium which forms the principal constituent of this preparation. You may not be aware that in addition to its medicinal purposes, this chemical is an excellent conductor of heat – so much so, in fact, that it has been used to contain and extinguish fires, and it was this, I believed, that was responsible for the rapid extinction of the flames that had appeared.

"Of course, this still left the mystery of how the fire was started, and what method had been used to prepare the materials in a locked room. I determined once more not to follow Kirkwind's example, but to remain and reach the bottom of this mystery, for I was now convinced that Sir William had been the victim of foul play, and that even if a charge of murder could not be brought against his killer, given that his death could not be directly attributed to the fires and conflagrations in his room, some form of justice should be done.

"The rest of the day was a gloomy one. Since Sir James, as I will refer to him from now on, had taken up residence in the King's Room, that avenue of exploration was closed to me, and I was forced to fall back on my own resources, and those of the library for occupation. The latter proved a poor source of distraction, consisting chiefly of country histories and sermons dating from the last century, and I turned with some relief to one of the volumes I had brought with me, dealing with some of the occult and esoteric practices that are carried out in India by the various cults and sects there.

"I dined alone, Sir James still remaining in his room, and I retired early to bed in the Blue Room.

"You will scarcely credit it, but once more I was awakened by Simmons in the early morning requesting my urgent attendance in the King's Room. 'It's Sir James, sir,' he cried.

" 'Why? Is he dead?' I asked.

" 'No, sir, but he's at death's door, in my opinion. Williams has gone to fetch Doctor Kirkwind. I am afraid I could not help but overhear what you two gentlemen were talking about yesterday, but I do trust that the doctor will remember his obligations to those in need.'

" 'So do I,' I answered him, throwing on my dressing-gown and following the butler to the now familiar chamber, where Sir James lay, pale and panting as if exhausted by running a long race. Though I am not a medical man, I have seen enough in my time to make it clear to me that I was in the presence of one who had not long to live.

" 'Water,' he croaked, and I hastened to pour from the carafe into a glass and hold it to his lips. 'Is the doctor coming? Kirkwind, damn him?'

"I was struck by the imprecation, but hastened

to assure him that help was being sought, and would probably not be too long in arriving. Sir James sighed, and lay back against the pillow.

"I waited for thirty minutes – and my God, they were along the longest thirty minutes of my life. If you can put yourselves in my position, seated beside a man who was obviously at death's door, a man who had been as good as accused by his own doctor of murdering his own brother, waiting for that same doctor to make an appearance – either to kill as a result of the hatred he bore towards his patient, or to follow his Oath and attempt to cure him.

"At length Kirkwind made his entrance. He would have made a consummate actor, I thought to myself, as I watched his face, which appeared to radiate nothing but kindly concern. 'Now let's have you up and about, old man,' he said, in the most considerate and soothing of tones. 'It's nothing but the effects of the last day or so that have laid you low.'

"For answer, Sir James spat out a foul epithet, which I will not trouble myself to repeat here. Kirkwind paid no attention, but produced a couple of tablets which he extended to Sir James. 'Heart,' he mouthed to me, almost silently. 'Family weakness. Digitalis.' Although the patient appeared reluctant to swallow the drug, Kirkwind persisted, and the tablets were duly swallowed. Kirkwind took himself to the other side of the room, and seated himself by the window at the foot of the bed.

"As I watched, Sir James's breathing became even more erratic, and his lips took on a bluish tinge. I made as if to call out to Kirkwind, but he held out a hand, signifying, I suppose, that these symptoms were to be expected. Simmons entered, followed by a maid, bearing a tray with tea and toast. 'I trust you gentleman will pardon my presumption in this matter, but I considered that you might require some refreshment. I have prepared three cups, but,' looking sadly at the recumbent figure in the bed, 'I fear only two will be required.'

"He poured the tea, and Kirkwind and I sat sipping from our cups, as Simmons and the maid stood by. The silence was suddenly broken by a harsh scream from Sir James.

" 'That, sir,' cried the dying man, struggling to rise from his deathbed, and pointing with a bony finger, 'That, sir, is the man who murdered my brother!'

A hushed silence followed this dread pronouncement, and all eyes turned towards the direction in which the finger pointed. We beheld Sir James, white-faced and gasping for breath, as he fell back, finger still outstretched to indicate the murderer. Kirkwind shrank back as if the mere pointing of a finger exerted a force against him.

"'It's a foul lie!' he shouted, but the impact of his words was lessened by two near-simultaneous sounds. The first was the unmistakable death-rattle uttered by Sir James as he collapsed lifeless upon the pillows. The second was a creaking groaning noise caused by the sliding aside of a section of the oak panelling that covered the walls of the room, disclosing a dark cavity, towards which Kirkwind made a dash.

"I am pretty quick on my feet, as you know, and I swiftly laid him by the heels. The good Simmons came to my aid, and he assisted me to convey the struggling physician to a chair, to which I bound him with the cord of my dressing-gown.

"'Go and tell one of the men to fetch the constable here,' I instructed the wide-eyed maid, 'and then bring ropes here to bind this man.'

"'There is no need for the ropes,' Kirkwind said sadly. 'I give you my word that I will not attempt to escape. Let me tell you all before the constable arrives.' Simmons made as if to leave, but Kirkwind bade him stay. 'You may as well hear the truth at first hand,' he said, 'rather than some garbled version at third- or fourth-hand. You know, of course, that he,' nodding at the body of Sir James, 'was in debt? Well, so was I. I had made some foolish investments on 'Change, and Sir William was kind enough to advance me some money to recoup my losses, money which I imagined I would be able to repay in a matter of weeks. Well, to cut a long story short, the weeks turned to months, and before I knew it, the months had turned to years, and I was no nearer restitution than I had been at the start. Then James returned, and he likewise was in debt to his brother, who had collected some, but not all, of his IOUs, and settled accounts with those creditors. A considerable amount was still outstanding, and the creditors were pressing.

" 'So now there were two of us who would stand to benefit if Sir William were out of the way. I knew, of course, that a weak heart was a family failing, but it was James who suggested the idea of bringing the old family curse into the business. He reasoned that if enough spontaneous unexplained fires were to occur, harmless enough in themselves, Sir William's heart would give out, and no-one would be able to prove that his demise was anything other than a natural death.

'As you know, Sir William slept soundly through the first fires, but the two last fires, set on his very pillow a matter of inches from his head, were enough to wake him, and cause his heart to give out. I may console you,' addressing the shocked and stricken Simmons, 'with the knowledge that his death would have been swift and almost painless.'

"'I understand how you prevented the fires from spreading,' I said to him, 'by the use of hydroxide of magnesium spread in a circle around the source of the fire. As soon as the flames reached the substance, all heat would be taken away, and the fire would die, in the way I myself witnessed. But how were the fires started?'

"Kirkwind bowed his head. 'Congratulations on your perception, Carnacki. The fires were started by means of a small grain of white phosphorus, wrapped in wet cotton-wool. When the water evaporated, which it did in a matter of hours, the phosphorus started a small fire inside the cotton-wool, which then spread to the surface on which it was placed, and was then presented from going further by the ring of hydroxide of magnesium spread around it. The phosphorus was placed by James, of course, using the passage between his room and this, which historians believe was constructed for the King to make an unobserved escape in the event of an attack by the Roundheads. It may be opened from either end, as I did just now using this concealed lever, and is, as you have seen for yourselves, nearly invisible when it is closed. Since the door of this room was constantly locked, and it was believed that James kept to his bed, no-one was able to discover the source of the fires.'

" 'And...?' I indicated the inert body on the bed.

" 'He had become tiresome. He had informed me that when he had inherited the title and the estate, he had no intention of forgiving my debts, but would press for repayment with the full rigour of the law. I could see no other option but to rid myself of him. But I had no idea it would all occur this way. His sudden collapse last night was, I am sure, a perfectly natural event. I swear am innocent of that, however much I may have hastened his end with that final dose of digitalis.'

"At this point the constable arrived, and I gave Kirkwind in charge, giving a brief account of the facts that Kirkwind had related, and signifying my willingness to act as a witness should this be required. Simmons likewise offered his testimony, and Kirkwind was led away, almost with a look of relief on his face, as if a weight had been lifted from his should, which in a way I suppose it had.

"And now I come to the queerest part of my tale. The body of James Offley was removed from the bed, and it was revealed that under the head and body, upon the sheets, there were no fewer than six scorched circles of the form that had previously been caused by the phosphorus bombs that had so terrified Sir William. I naturally examined them closely, but in none of them could

I discover the magnesium compound that had arrested the fires in the past. Indeed, the edges of the charred circles formed a clean break between black and white, unlike the previous circle I had observed, which went from black through several shades of grey before it reached the unburned white cotton of the pillow. The burned patch itself seemed more even than previously.

"What was the cause? I asked myself. Kirkwind had told us that he had not set these fires, and it was hardly likely that James Offley would have set them himself. To what end or benefit? Then I had a thought, and a very strange one it was, too. Perhaps, I reasoned, I was responsible for these scorched circles, not directly, you understand, but through my muddles and meddling. You know that whenever any part of the Saaamaaa Ritual is performed, it attracts the attention of the Others. This, together with the force of James Offley's hate, and the terror of his brother, may have summoned the Aeiirii. In the book about Indian cults that I was reading earlier in the library, it described the feats of some yogis or native priests, who are reputed to summon Hindoo demons, or Rakshasha, through the power of their emotions. I believe that I was responsible for opening the gate, and James Offley and Kirkwind between them unwittingly performed the actual summoning of the Aeiirii.

"I cannot say that I feel any regret over the arrest of Kirkwind, who behaved as no man should and will, if there is any justice, hang. Nor can I shed tears over James Offley. But I failed miserably and wretchedly when it came to the protection of Sir William Offley, and the memory of my failure will remain with my to my death."

He ceased to speak, and there was silence for a few minutes, broken only by the rattle of coals in the grate, and a faint shuffle as one of us moved in a chair.

At length the silence was broken by Carnacki himself.

"Out you go!" he commanded us, invoking the usual formula.

The story that rewrote itself

USUALLY I write using a computer. But the other night, I couldn't be bothered to go into the room where I keep the computer, turn the thing on, and write down the thoughts that had occurred to me. So I started to write longhand, with a pen – and I don't mean a ballpoint pen. This was a fountain pen, filled with turquoise ink.

[Why turquoise? you ask. Simple – the local stationery store was having a closing-down sale, and they were selling bottles of turquoise ink for 10p. So...]

Anyway, I wrote and I wrote, and I went to bed, and in the night something very strange happened. Don't ask me how I knew all of this – I would have said it was a dream, except for all that I saw the next morning, but it did seem to me that I was watching all this from my bed as it happened.

I'd created words, and the order and

association of these words had created meaning, and it seemed to me somehow that the words didn't like the meaning and the uses to which I'd put them, so they flew off the page like a flock of turquoise kingfishers, and started rearranging themselves into the patterns and meanings that they preferred.

Taking off in turn, the words somehow detached themselves from the page, and circled around before arriving back on the page with a an audible "plop". Sometimes they didn't seem to land in quite the right place, and they shuffled along the line to their rightful positions with a squelching sound.

I wasn't close enough to them to see their identity or what they were trying to write, but it seemed that they were constantly in a state of flux, changing places with each other, and sometimes leaving the paper to let their place be taken by another. Some scarlet word-birds flew in from time to time to take the place of the kingfishers, which flapped off, sighing regretfully.

I watched, fascinated, as they manoeuvred themselves into what turned out to be their final resting places, and all movement stopped.

In the morning, I wasn't sure if I had dreamed all this or not, and I went downstairs to see the piece of paper that I had left on the table the night before. It certainly wasn't what I had written

– though I recognised a lot of the words. But some, in red, were words that I didn't remember writing, and the ones that I did remember writing were not in the order that I remembered.

And what was the writing? you ask. Well, that's yet another story. I left the piece of paper on the table all day, almost frightened to touch it, given the changes that had gone on the previous night. When I went to bed that night, I was on the verge of dropping off to sleep, when I "saw" the paper on the table once more. As I watched, all the kingfisher-blue and all the cardinal-red word-birds took off, and flew up to the ceiling, where they slowly melted away into nothingness.

This time, I didn't wait till the morning. I rushed downstairs, and found – a blank piece of paper.

And what had been on it? My words had transformed themselves into a story, or to be more accurate, a description, of the nameless horrors that lurk at the edges of our consciousness and slither into our nightmares. I am thankful that I can no longer remember the details, but I can only assume that the words were so horrified by what they had become that they decided to annihilate themselves and leave our world unaware of the terrors on the other side of the veil.

Gianni Two-Pricks

GIOVANNI was the proud possessor of two penises.

One, uncircumcised, shyly poked its head from a mass of black curls between his thighs. It had always been his. The other hung from a gold chain around his neck. It was well above average size, circumcised, and had the appearance and texture of a piece of leather. This one had not originally been Giovanni's, but had been taken by him from the body of a Barbary pirate who had made the mistake of attacking the Genoese galley on which Giovanni served as a soldier. Others from Giovanni's crew collected ears, and the less sentimental of them simply stripped the dead of their golden rings and earrings, but Giovanni had noticed his dead opponent's anatomy when the body was stripped of its garments prior to being thrown into the sea, and decided to take it as a souvenir. As an afterthought, he had also stripped off the gold chain from around the pirate's neck. It was this chain from which his prize now dangled.

He made no secret of his trophy, once he had suitably treated it using skills from his former occupation as a tanner, and converted it into an ornament. The rest of the crew and soldiers on the *San Giorgio*, the galley on which he served, started to call him by the name "Gianni Two-Pricks", and later just "Two-pricks", an appellation to which he answered with pride.

When the galley put into port, his new name always caused baffled amusement among those who heard it in the taverns when it was shouted out by his shipmates. Usually, he had to unbutton his jerkin and show the assembly the source of his nickname. Later, he often found a willing bed partner to whom he could display the second half of his new name.

A few months after he had started to wear his trophy, Two-pricks started to dream. It was always the same dream on two or three successive nights, after which he would sleep dreamlessly for a few more nights before the dream started again.

In the dream, he was with a beautiful girl, who took him to a room with a soft bed, started to caress him, and gradually removed all her clothes before starting to undress him. At the end, when she removed his breeches, she shrieked with terror, and fled, naked, out of the room. In his dream, Two-pricks looked down between his legs to see a bleeding stump where his penis should have been. At this point in the dream, he invariably woke up, streaming with sweat, and fumbling desperately between his legs to ensure that the dream was not a reality.

His messmates were sometimes awakened by his nocturnal adventures, and repeated, with exaggerations, the noises he had been making, starting with erotic moans, and changing to screams of absolute terror, though they had no idea of the content of his dreams – Two-pricks never told anyone. Even more terrifying to Two-pricks was the fact that he found himself impotent whenever he found himself with a woman in real life. In his mind, the woman before him became the girl in his dreams, and he dreaded the moment when it the time came for him to draw off his breeches, knowing that his member would remain flaccid and useless, no matter what methods of persuasion were used to make it stand upright.

Eventually, he ceased even making an attempt to go with his shipmates in search of women, and remained at the tavern, drinking until he could no longer stand, and had to be carried back to the *San Giorgio* by his friends. He could not talk to anyone about his problems – his drinking companions would merely laugh at him, and the idea of going to the priest in order that he might be able to commit fornication again... Two-pricks (how he had come to hate that name) shook his head, and downed another goblet of rough red wine.

That night, in his alcohol-fuelled stupor, before he went to sleep, Two-pricks removed the chain from around his neck, and wrapped it carefully inside the rolled jerkin that served him as a pillow. He spent the night without dreaming, and the next night and the night after that, after removing the chain and his trophy before retiring for the night. In fact, a whole week went by without these dreams. Even so, the memory of the previous terrors stuck with him, and he still feared the humiliation that he knew was inevitable if he were to visit a woman.

And then the second series of dreams began. In them, Two-pricks was naked, other than for a flimsy white shirt. His hands were tied behind his back, and he was being led out of a city to a place that he knew was a place of execution. How or why he was to be executed, he had no idea, though the guards on either side of him were laughing and making rough jokes that he could barely understand, at his expense.

Then they reached the place of execution, and the full horror of the situation hit him. However many times he dreamed the dream, the method by which he was to be killed burst upon him anew in hideous detail.

A large iron pole in the shape of a phallus stood upright in the middle of a clearing. Two-pricks was to be impaled on that pole, and he knew that he would die in fearful agony as he struggled and his body was ripped apart from the inside by the sharp iron teeth he could now see embedded in the surface of the instrument of torture.

Invariably, as the guards lifted him up, and his body prepared for the agony of the metal penis entering his flesh, he woke up. Usually the straw on which he lay was soaked with his urine, and on more than one occasion, fouled with his ex-crement. Of course this attracted the attention of his shipmates, and after ordering him for the sixth time to clean up after himself, they insisted that he make his bed a long way from the oth-ers – indeed, they ordered him, with blows and curses, to sleep on the foul-smelling benches of the galley slaves, many of whom were of the same race as the unfortunate who had unknowingly been the source of Two-pricks' trophy.

Here he felt himself to be in danger – he was one of the hated enemy, and he was convinced that despite their chains and manacles, the slaves would kill him if they could. He dared not take the chain with the trophy from around his neck, and the dreams of impalement continued, in-creasing in their intensity and terror. Although he tried to keep alert in his perilous situation, he needed to sleep from time to time, and after dropping off on one of these occasions, he woke to discover his scabbard empty, and the dagger which it had contained gone.

Though he raged up and down the slave benches, swearing furiously, and dealing out cuffs and buffets to the unfortunate wretches who, chained as they were, could not avoid the blows, he was unable to locate the dagger. To his fury, the slave-master, who by all rights should have been supporting him in his quest for his stolen property, simply sat and laughed at him.

By now, Two-pricks wanted nothing so much as to cast his ghastly trophy into the sea, but try as he might, he found himself unable to undo the clasp of the chain that held the dead man's penis. All his appeals for help failed to raise a response. Very well, then, he decided, he would simply tear the loathsome object from the chain, but again, he failed to do so. His skill as a tanner, and the exposure to the salt sea air had made the skin harder than the toughest shoe leather, and it was impossible to tear it loose.

Without his dagger, he was unable to cut through the leather, and in a fury, he stormed up to the slave-master and demanded the use of the latter's blade. Smiling mockingly, the slave-master shook his head in silent refusal. An appeal to his former comrades for the loan of their weapons was greeted by hail of stale breadcrusts, and a rain of the contents of the piss-buckets.

Wet and stinking, Two-pricks made his way to the deck, where he stood on the forecastle, tears of anger and shame running down his face. His hand brushed against a barrel containing arrows, and he picked one up, with the idea that he could use the sharpened edge of the steel arrow-head to cut through the leather.

He raised the arrow to his throat, but before he could make his move, the *San Giorgio* lurched to larboard as a gust of wind coincided with a larger than usual wave on the starboard bow. The steel pierced his throat, slicing through a vein, and with a gurgling cry, Two-pricks sank to the deck, from which he fell into the sea as the *San Giorgio* rolled with the next wave.

Some of the crew watched helplessly as the galley, unable to stop, swept past him on her way to meet the Ottoman fleet at Lepanto. Though they threw ropes towards Two-pricks, he seemed unconscious of their actions, and made no attempt to catch them. They watched, crossing themselves, as he went down for the third time, a mysterious green haze arising from the spot where he was last seen.

To this day, it is said that no ship can cross the spot where Two-Pricks breathed his last without the male members of the crew experiencing an abrupt stabbing pain in their genitals, which lasts for a matter of some minutes before departing as suddenly and mysteriously as it arrives.

Lady of the Dance

THE moon cast inky shadows of the olive trees surrounding the temple on the stone-flagged pavement in front of the ruined gateway. As Helena entered the grove, she could hear the faint rustle of leaves in the breeze.

She turned towards the gateway, opened her mouth, and shut it again with no words spoken. The time for speech was not now.

Bending down, she unfastened her sandals and kicked them off, sending them spinning into the undergrowth beneath the trees. The heat from the stones, still warm after a day of Mediterranean sun, shot through the soles of her bare feet, and she gave a little gasp. Her T-shirt and shorts followed her sandals, and she paused stock still, head bowed, seemingly lost in thought. At last, she reached up and unhooked her bra, and wriggled out of her panties. Now she was ready.

She dropped to her knees and gazed at the weathered carvings, over three thousand years old, depicting a woman, as naked as Helena was now, facing a creature that seemingly was not of this world, a creature all tentacles and eyes. She stared at the ancient scene for almost five minutes before rising slowly to her feet, stretching her legs, and preparing herself for what was to come.

A multitude of drummers began to play inside her head, combining and conflicting rhythms in a whirlwind of sound. Beneath this symphonic cacophony she could make out one pulsing beat, and her body started to respond to it. She extended one foot, her toes with their painted toenails moving slightly to the inaudible rhythm. Her hands started to twitch, and then the other foot started to move. A step forward. One back. Two to the side, hands above her head, weaving a pattern that had been lost for centuries.

A spin. A half-turn. Stamp. Spin. Jump. Arms still forming the ancient symbol. Despite the cool night air, Helena felt herself starting to sweat.

The drums beat faster and her pace quickened to join them. Leaping, prancing, spinning. Step right. Spin. Move left three steps. Jump. Every move was pre-ordained, part of a message that came from deep within herself. A message, centuries old, that she had always known, but she had never been aware of the knowledge until now.

Sweat now poured down her body, and her hair whipped across her face. Exhausted, but this was no time to stop. Turn. Jump. Step. Slide back.

Her eyes moved to the gateway. Was that her imagination, or was that a crack in the floor between the pillars? Spin. Stamp. Jump. The crack seemed to grow wider. Step right. Step left. Circle. Hop. And out of the crack came something darker than the olive trees' shadows, something that had a quality of absolute blackness about it, and yet seemed to glow with a black light.

Exhausted, Helena ceased her dance and sank to the ground. The Message of Summoning had been sent and received.

"Master," she whispered.

Me and my Shadow

WHAT happened last night helped me make up my mind. I am not going to walk around Stowe Pool at night ever again.

I wasn't planning to walk, but I was going to take the car because I was feeling lazy and somewhat pushed for time, but when I tried to start the car, I found the battery had gone flat. So I was in a bad mood as I set off, and it didn't get any better when I turned on my phone to try to listen to some music, and found that the batteries had gone flat on that, as well.

The wind was blowing, and though it wasn't actually raining, it seemed as though it would start soon. Why was I doing this? I asked myself. I could get up early the next morning and drop the form through my friend's letterbox then. Except, of course, I knew I couldn't. I don't get up early. So I strode on, picturing myself as Scott of the Antarctic heroically striding through the blizzard.

There was no-one else stupid enough to be

walking the path around the Pool, and the ducks and seagulls seemed to have gone to bed for the night. I turned off the path, up the street, and rang my friend's doorbell. As I had expected, there was no answer. I'd sort of expected that, so I dropped the note that I'd written earlier through the door together with the form, asking him to sign the form and drop it in the post.

And then it was time for the return trip. Down towards the Pool, and I decided to go round the other way, down towards St Chad's and up the other side. The moon was shining through the clouds, and the two spires of the cathedral turned to three as I reached the end of the Pool. There's something rather comforting about having a cathedral watching over you, I thought to myself, but then–

I stumbled over a branch which had broken off a tree, and as I recovered my balance, I looked down at the Pool. There was someone lying there, and I scrambled down the bank to see if they were all right. All I had seen was a dark shadowy figure – I couldn't even tell if it was a man or a woman lying there, but whoever it was, they needed help. Their head appeared to be just about in the water, and there seemed to be some danger of them drowning. The ground was muddy, and I slipped down the bank, even though I was watching my steps carefully. But when I reached the bottom of the bank, picked myself up, and looked, the figure had vanished.

I'd been deceived by a trick of the light, I told myself. I'd seen my own shadow as if it was a real person. I swore to myself and climbed back up again. There was the figure by the pool again, and there was a streetlight shining from the road behind me. So that was all I'd seen – my shadow. I proved it to myself by waving both my hands in the air, and the shadowy figure waved as well. I put my hands down – but the figure didn't – its hands were still up in the air. I raised my hands above my head, and the figure did the same. My eyes were playing tricks on me. I rubbed them, and put my hands down by my side, but the figure kept its hands up. Then one of its hands fell by its side, and it waved with the other as it seemed to move slowly away from me.

You know how your shadow moves and changes size and shape when it's a car or something moving that's making the shadow with its headlights? Well, that's exactly what it looked like, but there were no cars around. Then the figure stood up on the water. Not in the water – on it. I could see its feet resting on the surface. There were no features visible, just a grey shape. Then it turned away from me, and started walking across the water, towards the Cathedral end of the Pool. At one point, I thought I could see its face, but then I realised that I was looking through this thing at some trees behind it.

Was I frightened? I was scared witless. You may think it's a cliché when someone describes the hairs on the back of their neck standing on end, but that's what happened to me. I stood there, too frightened to move until I lost sight of the thing, and then I ran. I didn't run home. I ran to the nearest pub, and downed a double straight whisky. I don't even like whisky, but I needed that.

At least no-one said to me, "You look as though you've seen a ghost." But to be honest with you, I have no idea what I saw, and I tell you, I'm not going to put myself in a position where I will see it again.

What happens afterwards?

THEY couldn't save me. I watched them as they worked on my body on the operating table. The cancer had gone too far, the surgeon told his team. They could keep me alive, but...

"Don't do it!" I screamed inaudibly at them. "1 don't want more months of agony. Just make a small mistake with the anaesthetic or something."

I knew he couldn't have heard me, but right on cue, the anaesthetist pushed a few buttons on his control panel, and my body's breathing slowed. The gaps between the beeps from the heartrate monitor started to get longer and longer.

The surgical team carried on, and the surgeon said something to them that I couldn't catch. Then there were no more beeps, and a nurse stepped towards the operating table with something that I seemed to recognise as a defibrillator, but the surgeon waved her back.

"It wouldn't be doing him any favours," he told her.

Good man. At least someone understood the

problems here.

And now I was free. Instead of being tied to my body, I could move around. I stationed myself behind the nurse who had tried to revive me and tapped her on the shoulder. I can't say how I managed that, because of course I had no hands or limbs. It worked, though. She turned to see who had touched her, and saw no-one. She shivered. "Ugh!"

"Someone walk over your grave, Sandra?" one of the other nurses asked her.

"Felt like it," she answered. Closer to the truth than she knew, I suppose.

I made my way to London, where I found my way (don't ask me how, because it all seemed so natural that it didn't need any explanation) to the house of a politician whom I had loathed and despised for years. I discovered him lolling on a sofa, a glass of red wine by his side, stuffing his face with peanuts and watching "Eastenders".

Could I? I could. His glass toppled over and spilled the contents all over the nice cream sofa.

"Susan!" he yelled, half-rising. "Cloth!"

I managed to overturn the bowl of peanuts, and let him grind them into the white carpet with his feet while he waited for Susan and the cloth.

"You're so bloody careless," she said to him as she came in.

"I never touched it. It just fell over by itself."

"Ha! With the bottle half-empty, you expect me to believe that?"

This had all the makings of a nice little domestic row, and I was just about to settle myself down and enjoy the show, when I felt a tap on my own shoulder (or what would have been my shoulder if I had one).

"Time to go," the angel told me. "Not that this doesn't look like fun, and I agree he deserves all he's getting now, and worse, but your time's up."

"Where are we going?"

"Where the hell do you think?" the angel said, and laughed.

About the Author

HUGH Ashton was born in the United Kingdom, and moved to Japan in 1988, where he lived until his return to the UK in 2016.

He is best known for his Sherlock Holmes stories, which have been hailed as some of the most authentic pastiches on the market, and have received favourable reviews from Sherlockians and non-Sherlockians alike.

He has also published other work in a number of genres, including alternative history, historical science fiction, and thrillers, based in Japan, the USA and the UK

He currently lives in the historic city of Lichfield with his wife, Yoshiko.

His ramblings may be found on Facebook, Twitter, and in various other places on the Internet. He may be contacted at: author@HughAshtonBooks.com

The Adventure of the Bloody Steps
The Adventure of Vanaprastha (ebook only)

There are also children's detective stories, with beautiful illustrations by Andy Boerger, the first of which was nominated for the prestigious Caldecott Prize :

Sherlock Ferret and the Missing Necklace
Sherlock Ferret and The Multiplying Masterpieces
Sherlock Ferret and The Poisoned Pond
Sherlock Ferret and the Phantom Photographer
The Adventures of Sherlock Ferret

There are also short stories, thrillers, alternative history, and historical science fiction titles:

Tales of Old Japanese
At the Sharpe End
Balance of Powers
Beneath Gray Skies
Red Wheels Turning
Angels Unawares
The Untime
The Untime Revisited

Full details of all of these and more at :
https://HughAshtonBooks.com

www.ingramcontent.com/pod-product-compliance
Lightning Source LLC
Chambersburg PA
CBHW031032190726
48286CB00003BA/1136